Diary of Steve the Noob 4

Steve the Noob

Thank You

Thank you for picking up a copy of my book. I spent many hours putting this book together, so I hope that you will enjoy reading it. As a Minecraft player, it brings me great joy to be able to share my stories with you. The game is fun and entertaining, and surprisingly, writing about it can be almost just as fun. Once you are done reading this book, if you enjoyed it, please take a moment to leave a review. It will help other people discover this book. If after reading it, you realize that you hate it with such passion, please feel free to leave me a review anyway. I enjoy reading what people think about my books and writing style. I hope that many people will like this book and encourage me to keep writing. Thanks in advance.

Special thanks to readers of my previous books. Thank you for taking the time to leave a review. I appreciate it so much; your support means so much to me. I will continue to keep writing and will try to provide the highest quality of unofficial Minecraft books. Thank you for your support.

I apologize to my readers for releasing this volume so late. School started so I got a bit distracted and a couple of other things came up, but everything should be good now. I'll get back to publishing new books regularly. Once again, I apologize for the delay.

Check Out My Author Page

Steve the Noob

My Other Books

Diary of Steve the Noob

Diary of Steve the Noob 2

Friday

Hmm…Let's see…where did I leave off?

Oh, yeah! This gigantic slime cube was chasing me down!

BOOM!!

BOOM!!

Every time the giant jelly landed, it created earthquakes throughout the land. The loud impact of his landing was enough to make my ears ring.

Ugh! This is so annoying, I thought to myself. *He is big, so he is pretty slow. I know I can outrun him, but every time that big o' cube lands, I lose my balance and fall to the ground. Then he catches up to me and we start all over again.*

Think, Steve! Think!

Oh, wait, I know! I'll just have to jump right before he lands. If I time it perfectly, I will miss out on the shock wave completely.

Okay, time to give this a try…

BOOM!!

Whooaa…gah! I fell over, but quickly picked myself up.

Okay, I wasn't ready yet…Let's count it out.

1…

2…

3…

Jump!

BOOM!!

HAHAHA! It worked! I didn't topple over from the tremors.

Now that I have this figured out, I can safely get away from this super cube. But where can I go? I can't go home. What if he follows me home and stomps on the whole village?

No, no…that just won't do. Then it will become the second village I've destroyed! Yikes…I surely don't want that on my resume…

Ahhh! Think, Steve! What are you gonna do???

I proceeded to run and jump for the next 30 minutes, but the fear of getting stomped on and running for my life really took a toll on me. I guess the stress of all that caused me to yell out, "Whyyy?! Why me?!"

Then…

A slow, loud, booming voice filled the air.

"You…"

I was in shock. *Where was that coming from?!* I thought to myself. *Could it be from the giant slime?*

"You…bad…"

"Whaaaaat?! You can talk?!" I shouted back while running and jumping.

"I big slime! I big brain!"

"Pffftahahaha! What!?"

I probably shouldn't have laughed at the way he spoke, but I did…and I think it made him mad.

The big slime took an extra big jump and landed extra hard. It totally threw off my timing and I fell to the ground. He got way too close to me…

"Gahh…W-wait…can't we talk about this?" I pleaded.

"Talk? Talk bout whut?" he replied with his rumbling voice. "You hurt our young ones. You bad. Now I keel you!"

Waaaaahhhhh! I got up and started running again.

BOOM!!

BOOOOOM!!

He is jumping and landing more sporadically. It is totally throwing me off, but if I watch him carefully and jump at the right time, I should be able to still avoid the shock wave.

"I go boom-boom! You go doom-doom!" he said menacingly.

OMG. His threats are so funny, but extremely scary as well. I can't keep running forever through these plains. I have to escape him somehow…

"I turn you into pancake! HAR! HAR! HAR!" he said and laughed.

HUFF! PUFF! "C-come on…can't we…talk about…this? I-I'm sorry…" I replied breathlessly.

"Too late, now you pancake."

It was starting to get late in the day. The night was going to be upon us soon. I wondered if he had bad night vision. Maybe I could escape him then, but I was so exhausted from running. I couldn't go on for much longer.

Could this be the end of Steve the noob? Am I destined to become a pancake from getting stomped on mercilessly? I thought to myself.

Then it came to me…

The perfect idea…

I had been digging holes all this time. Holes have been my savior and will be once again!

I got a good amount of distance away from the big slime. Then I proceeded to dig a quick hole as deep as I could. I was only able to go down a few blocks until I hit bedrock, but it was enough to cover myself up.

Alright! Whew! I can just hide in here and catch a breather, I thought to myself.

But soon, the green meanie approached. He landed right above my hole.

BOOM!!!

BOOOOOOM!!!

"I see you, pancake!"

Ahhhhhhhhh! The shock wave is so powerful when I'm right at the center of it.

"I keel you!! Har! Har! Har!"

Okay, this is totally not going to work. I won't be able to rest like this, not with him bouncing right above my head.

BOOOM!!

BOOOM!!

Alright, I can't dig down any further, but I can still dig sideways. Hmm...that's a good idea. I can dig myself a tunnel and then pop out somewhere far away from this jerk. HAHAHA! Steve, you're a genius!

So, I dug for a few minutes. I got rattled a few times in the tunnel from the shock waves. It made me super dizzy, and I was so glad I'm wasn't a claustrophobic type of person. Soon, the tremors were getting weaker and weaker as I gained more distance from the super cube.

I dug one block up and popped out of the tunnel. I looked back to see the giant cube stomping relentlessly on the hole I was in. He looked like he was having fun. *What a jerk,* I thought.

Okay, now that I've escaped, what am I going to do? I guess I should head back to town and consult the mayor and villagers.

When I approached the village, I could see everyone standing outside, looking into the direction of the cube monster. I was happy to see everyone again, but I also noticed the terror in their eyes. Everyone seemed surprised to see me.

I hopped over the trench and was immediately greeted by the mayor.

"Steve! We all thought you were dead!" the mayor yelled.

"Oh, no, not yet. That thing almost got me, but I'm just a little bit too slick," I replied.

"Okay, good, because from far away, it looked like that thing was stomping on you and blending you into the grass."

I laughed. "Ah, yeah, I dug a hole to hide in and used it as my escape."

"Good thinking, Steve. While you were off running around and evading that monster, the villagers and I have been deciding on how to handle the situation."

"Oh, that's great! Did you all figure something out?"

"Yes…"

"What is it?"

"We've decided to abandon the village and run for our lives! We don't wanna get smushed!"

"What?! You must be joking."

"Well, we all thought you were dead, and we're pretty much defenseless against such a monster. What else could we do?"

I was quiet for a moment, and then I turned to the crowd of villagers. "As the defender of this village, I will promise I will defeat this monster somehow. I'll destroy him and we won't have to run away from our homes."

Everyone cheered reluctantly.

"Since Steve is still alive, I guess we do have a chance," the mayor added.

"You bet! I've been thinking of a plan on my way over here," I said.

The crowd started looking more hopeful.

Bob joined the conversation. "What is your plan, Steve?"

"If my plan is to work, I will need the help of the entire village," I said.

The mayor was extremely eager to help. "No problem, Steve. Just tell us what you need and we'll make it happen."

"Okay, awesome. We're gonna have to work throughout the night, so get your tools and crafting kits ready."

Everyone nodded.

There was no point in trying to sleep that night anyway. With the colossal cube jumping up and down creating earthquakes, it was impossible to sleep. That night, we all gathered at the mayor's house.

I showed everyone my plan and explained how it should be crafted.

"Wow! This is a great idea, Steve!" yelled the mayor. "How did you come up with this?"

"Oh, as I was running throughout the day, I learned a lot about the enemy. I decided that the best way to fight it is to use its own force against it."

"Genius…pure genius, Steve," Bob added.

"Thanks, Bob! It should be fairly easy to make, and I have most of the material here in my bag."

"Okay, let's get started then," the mayor said.

We crafted throughout the night, and we made dozens of these items.

"The sun should be coming up soon. While we still have the cover of darkness, we should place some of our finished items out in the fields," I said. "Everyone else should continue crafting."

Everyone looked at each other with scared eyes.

"I need a volunteer to help me place these in the fields…Anyone?" I asked.

There was no answer and everyone's head was down.

I looked at the mayor, but he wasn't looking at me. He looked rather super busy crafting the items. He was working at like triple pace at that moment.

Then I looked at Bob.

Bob met my eyes and said…

"Uh, I gotta go pee…BRB…"

Oh, Bob! I can't believe he left me hanging like that…it seems like no one wants to help me place down the first batch. I can't possibly get it done all by myself, I thought.

Then a sweet and pretty voice came out of nowhere.

"I-I'll go with you, Steve…"

I turned around and saw Cindy smiling and slightly trembling.

"No, it is too dangerous, Cindy. I will do it by myself."

"Don't be silly, you can't place all of these before sunrise. I'm coming with you," she said sternly.

I was quiet for a moment. I wasn't sure of what to do, but I definitely needed the extra help. "Fine, but promise me you'll be careful and stay nearby."

She smiled. "Y-yes…of course!"

Though she was smiling, I could tell she was fearful of our task. We had to venture outside in the dark and place these things all over the place. At the same time, we must be very careful not to get the attention of the huge monster. There's no telling what could happen out there.

"Okay, Cindy, here's the plan."

She nodded.

"Because there are a bunch of monsters roaming around, the only safe way we could get around is by going underground," I said and I gave her a shovel. "We'll dig tunnels side by side and place the items topside along the way."

"Okay, Steve, I'm ready to go."

"Alright, everyone, wish us luck. We'll be back in a bit. Please keep crafting those things."

Everyone agreed and wished us luck.

Bob came back just in time to see us getting ready to leave.

"O-oh, h-hey, I'm back from the restroom. D-did you find a volunteer already? Oh, okay, darn, I-I'm too late...Good luck out there..." said Bob nervously.

"Oh, Bob..." I replied.

Cindy and I exited the mayor's house and headed towards the nearby trench. From there we dug tunnels towards the giant cube.

"Hey, Cindy!" I yelled through the dirt wall tunnel.

"Yeah?" she answered.

"If you need anything just yell, k? I'm only a few feet away."

She laughed. "Oh, you're worried about me, Steve?"

"Of course! I care about you."

"Y-you do...?"

I blushed. "A-ahem…I meant I care about your well-being."

"A-ah…right," she said shyly.

We proceeded to dig and placed the items until nearly sunrise with no incident.

Then suddenly I heard a sharp scream coming through the dirt.

AHHHHH!!!!

I smashed through the dirt wall to find Cindy cornered by a brain-hungry zombie.

"No worries, Cindy! I got you."

I pulled out my stone sword and drove it into the zombie.

Raggggghhhhh!

I whacked it a few more times until it dropped some rotten flesh.

"Whew! Thanks for saving me, Steve. I've never seen a zombie so up close before. They are actually quite stinky."

I laughed. "No problem. I'm here for you, Cindy."

She smiled.

"The sun will be up soon, we should probably head back," I said.

She nodded.

I stayed in her tunnel and led the way back.

On the way back, we encountered a baby zombie. That thing was lightning quick. The tunnel was narrow, so I couldn't really maneuver anywhere. No circle strafing technique for me.

Suddenly, I heard Cindy scream from behind me. I turned around to see another zombie behind her. It must have fallen through the holes we made topside.

Oh, no! We're trapped with nowhere to go! This isn't good, I thought to myself.

The baby zombie charged at me repeatedly with super speed. I held it off, but the zombie behind Cindy was getting closer. I wanted to help her right away, but I couldn't attack the other zombie without first striking her due to the tight tunnel space.

The regular zombie clawed Cindy and she screamed. I was still fighting the baby zombie.

Cindy fell over and the zombie got on top of her trying to bite her. She held it off with all her might.

"Ahh! Steve! Help me!" she yelled.

I turned around and saw an opening. I stabbed the zombie in the head.

The baby zombie took that opportunity to punch, kick, and bite me multiple times in the back. It hurt, but it wasn't too bad because of my full leather armor set.

When the regular zombie died, I turned around to finish off the baby zombie. I whacked it a few more times and then it poofed.

After that, I immediately tended to Cindy who was on the floor.

"Cindy! Are you okay?!" I yelled.

"O-o-ooh…" she murmured.

"Are you hurt?" I inspected her body for wounds. Then I saw something that made my heart sank. There were bite marks on her forearm.

She fell silent…

Oh, no! Cindy has been bitten! What do I do? What do I do?!

Her skin started to slowly turn green.

OMG! I think she's turning into a zombie! Nooooooooooooo! I don't want to kill my friend! What do I do?!

I thought for a moment, but with each passing second, her skin became greener.

Okay, I'm gonna drag her back into town. Maybe someone will know what to do.

I grabbed her and ran off towards town. I would have carried her, but there wasn't enough space in the tunnel.

When I arrived at the town trench, Bob and some villagers were already outside waiting for me.

"Hey! Steve and Cindy are back!" Bob yelled.

Then everyone gasped.

"What happened?!" Bob asked with great concern.

I dropped to my knees. "C-cindy...I think she got bitten...she might be...turning—"

"Hurry! Get her inside!" someone yelled.

I got up, picked her up in my arms, and ran towards my house.

"Put her inside and lock the door!" this person yelled to me.

I did so as quickly as I could. "Okay…done..." I was out of breath.

"Sorry, I didn't mean to yell. It is just that time was of the essence. The sun was starting to come up, and Cindy would have burned if you weren't quick enough."

"I see. Thanks for your helping. Is there anything else we can do for Cindy? There has to be a cure or something out there. "

"Maybe…I'm not quite sure. A witch might be able to tell you more."

"I see. Where can I find a witch?" I asked.

The mayor jumped in the conversation. "Steve, perhaps there are more dire things that require your attention during this time."

"But—"

"Now, we all love Cindy, but right now the whole town needs you," he explained.

"I know you're right, but I can't help it. I need to take care of Cindy right now. This is all my fault!"

"Cindy will be okay in your house," the stranger said to me.

"Are you certain? How do you know for sure?" I asked.

"I am the village librarian. I've read about these things before, though not extensively."

"I see. I apologize; I didn't mean to question you. Thanks for your help. I am Steve…the noob…"

"It is my honor to meet you, Steve. My name is Emily."

"Will you look after Cindy for me while I go take care of the slime monster?"

"I will. Don't worry about her, she'll be fine with me. Just focus on the task at hand."

"Thank you…" I said as I walked off slowly.

Saturday

The sun is up and shining now and my mind is torn in two. On the one side, I am about to enter the biggest battle of my life. On the other side, my conscience is guilt-ridden about what had happened to Cindy. I am completely torn apart. I don't know if I am capable of fighting right now.

"Cheer up, Steve. Cindy will be alright," said the mayor. Emily is our most knowledgeable villager, she will take good care of Cindy."

"Yeah, Steve, just focus on fighting the big slime. Cindy's condition can wait. If you don't handle the slime, he might destroy the whole village," said Bob.

I nodded along sadly.

"Steve, the needs of the many outweighs the needs of the few," added Lisa the elder.

"Come on, Steve. You're my hero! Go kick that slime's butt!" yelled Timmy the kid.

I looked up and saw everyone looking at me. Though I was sad, I felt motivated by their words and spirits. It was not the right time for me to be sad. I had to go handle business.

"Thank you, everyone. I needed your motivation and support. I will do my best in this upcoming battle," I said with some energy.

"Here, Steve. This is the rest of the batch that we crafted while you were gone," said Bob.

***

I guess I should take a moment to explain exactly what my plan was and what we've been crafting all night long.

The plan was simple. While running away from the giant slime, I studied its movement and behavior. I realized that because of its giant size, I probably wouldn't be able to hurt it very much by directly attacking it.

So, I decided that I will indirectly attack it by using a special item I invented. This special item will be called the Slime Ender.

Muahahaha! What a cool name!

Here it is, this is the Slime Ender...

It will use the enemy's natural movement and weight against the enemy.

I'm gonna get that slime so good!

To make it, I took a stone sword and a stone block and combined them with my crafting kit.

The plan was to craft a bunch of these and set them up all over the plains. Then I will go and provoke the monster and run away and drop off more Slime Enders along the way. He will jump and land on these and eventually kill himself.

It seemed like a pretty solid plan. Let's see how it plays out.

***

"Thank you, Bob. I guess I have everything and should head out now," I said.

Everyone wished me good luck.

As I headed out of town, I immediately spotted the giant cube.

To my surprise, he wasn't hopping up and down. It looked like he got tired and fell asleep.

I didn't even notice that the tremors stopped. I guess my mind was too occupied with other things.

As I approached him, I scattered more Slime Enders all over the place. I also tried my best to make a mental note of where most of the items were.

Before I knew it, I was close enough to hear the monster snore away.

Wow, it must be nice to be able to sleep whenever you want, I thought. *I guess he was exhausted from stomping on me all night.*

"Hey…" I said.

No response.

"HEY!" I yelled.

Still, nothing.

I grabbed a spare Slime Ender and threw it at the big slime. "Hey, slime jerk!"

It startled him awake. "HM!? Whut?!"

"It's me! Steve the slime basher!" I teased.

"You! How?!"

"I'm just too slick, puny," I replied and laughed.

"I not puny!" he yelled. "I da boss!"

"Ida? Isn't Ida a girl's name?" I laughed some more.

His eyebrows came down to an even sharper angle.

RAAAWWRRRR!!!

He jumped up and started chasing me.

I turned away and started running. "What? You mad, bro?"

BOOM!!!

BOOOM!!

Alright! It is working. I got him to chase me. Now, to lead him down to the Slime Ender traps, I thought to myself.

I ran and I ran. I was a bit nervous because I wasn't sure if the plan would work or not. As I ran, I thought of Cindy and I started feeling bad. In my distracted state of mind, I didn't see a rock on the ground and I tripped over it.

"Ooooof! Ugh…where did that rock come from?"

"HAHA! Now I gunna get ya!" the slime boss yelled.

He was closing the distance on me. I got up as quick as I could. I could see some Slime Enders not too far from where I was.

I gotta get there in time!

BOOOM!!

The tremors were getting louder and louder. He was right behind me.

Huff! Puff! Almost there!

"I gonna smush you good!" he threatened me.

"We'll see about that, slimey." I ran past the first Slime Ender.

Okay, let's see what happens.

Actually, he was so close behind me that I didn't even dare to look back.

And to my surprise, nothing happened…initially.

Hmm…no reactions? Gotta keep trying.

It turns out that he just happened to jump passed the first trap.

I ran towards the rest of the traps.

"MMMM…pancakes yummy!" he shouted.

"Hey, I like pancakes, too! Just not when I'm the pancake…"

"I make you flat-flat. Like this land!"

Huff! Puff! Ugh…I'm getting tired of sprinting. I need to get some rest soon. I hope these traps work or else I'll really become a pancake…

I ran past the other traps…

BOOM!!!

"OW!!"

BOOM!!!!

"OUCH!!!"

I looked back to see him slowing down. *Hahahaha! Looks like the traps worked. Well, I was hoping it would kill him, but slowing him down is good too*, I thought.

"Aww…what happened…why are you…so slow…?" I provoked as I was gasping for air.

"GRRR! I keel you!"

BOOOM!!

"OWWW!"

He landed on another Slime Ender.

Puhahahaha! The more he chases me, the more he hurts himself. This is hilarious.

"Hey…come on…I'm getting…bored here," I said.

He stood still for a bit.

"What…? Are you…tired? Do you…need some…food? Want some…pancakes?" I pestered.

He looked like he was thinking or something.

"Come on…Come at me, bro!" I yelled.

Suddenly, he crouched down low, then leaped high into the air towards me. I was taken by surprised. I didn't know he could jump that high or that far. He was projected to land right on top of me.

I jumped, tucked, and rolled out of his landing area. He missed me just by a hair.

Unfortunately for him, his landing area was full of Slime Enders.

The high jump resulted in a high impact. When he landed, his body compressed deeply on some Slime Enders. It punctured him more deeply than ever, and then he just fell over to his side.

The super jump caused a huge tremor, and I got rocked so badly. My brain felt like it was a marble in a shaking spray can. I couldn't move for a bit afterward.

When I finally gathered my composure, I looked to where the boss slime was.

He was knocked over with a bunch of drool coming out of his mouth.

I got up and looked around. "Ugh…I guess I did it…"

There were still a bunch of traps around, but they were all knocked over from the tremor. Then I heard something…

"I…go…"

I looked over at the slime boss.

"boom-boom…"

"You go doom-doom," I said as I walked away from him.

Then the slime boss exploded into hundreds of slimeballs.

I looked back. *Ah, I did it…finally…*

I was so exhausted from the battle that I just collapsed.

I must have laid there for a few minutes when suddenly a single word entered my mind: Cindy.

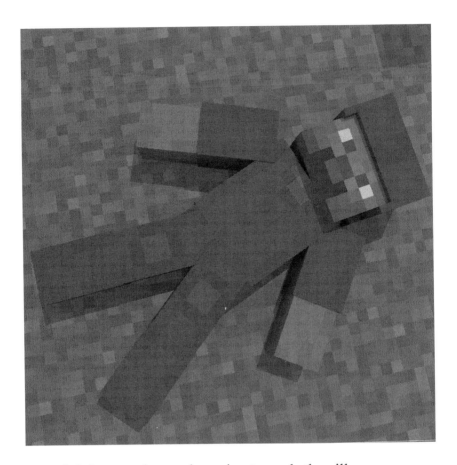

I popped right up and started running towards the village.

When I got closer to the village, I could see all the villagers standing outside cheering for me. Everyone was super excited and happy. They all wanted to congratulate me, but I ran right past them.

My legs were burning and my chest was on fire, but still I sprinted towards my house to see Cindy.

I arrived at my house to see Emily blocking my way.

"Stop, Steve," she said.

"What? Move out of the way, I need to see Cindy."

"You don't want to see her like this."

I moved around Emily and approached the door.

"Don't open it," she said strictly. "Don't go inside."

As I reached for the doorknob, the other villagers caught up to me.

"Stop, Steve. If you go inside, you'll expose Cindy to the sunlight," said Bob.

"But I—"

"He's right. Stay out here," added the mayor.

I was sad, but I knew everyone was right. So, I peeked through the window and in the corner, I saw a figure.

"Cindy?" I asked.

There was no response.

I knocked on the window. "Can you hear me, Cindy?"

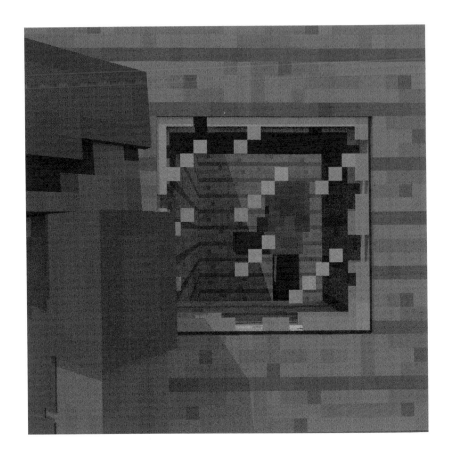

Nothing.

"It's me, Steve, your friend."

Then suddenly, the figure violently thrusted towards the window.

BANG!

Everyone gasped.

But I remained calm and looked at the figure with sad eyes.

"Omg…I'm so sorry, Cindy…"

Cindy had become a full blown zombie. Her skin was as green as the grass that surrounded us. She had no memories of her past.

"Cindy…I'm gonna fix this, I promise," I said as I lowered my head.

Emily approached me. "Steve, while you were gone, I got out some old books and did some research."

I looked up at her.

"According to the books, there is indeed a way to reverse the zombification."

"Really?!" I asked with excitement.

"Yes…"

"What is it?"

"Sorry, I don't know, the books didn't say."

"Aw…"

"But like I told you earlier, a witch might be able to tell you more about these things."

"Oh, that's right. I need to find a witch right away."

"Ah…lucky for you, Steve, there is one living nearby," Emily said.

"Really? Do you know her? Where is she?"

"Well, she used to be a villager living here, but one day she got struck by lightning and changed into a witch."

"Ah, yes, her…" the mayor added. "Her attitude changed greatly, so we had to remove her from this village. She wasn't too happy about that."

"I see," I said.

"She might be reluctant to help you due to that and due to another thing," Emily said.

I looked at Emily puzzled. "What other thing?"

"She is the—"

"Ahem! Let's not bring that up, Emily. It is not our place to say," interrupted the mayor.

"Ah, that's right. I'm sorry, Steve. This is something you'll need to learn on your own," said Emily to me.

"I see…okay. Where can I find her?"

"It is not too far away, you can find her hut to the east of the village. Her home will be hard to miss."

"Okay, I'm gonna head there now."

"Wait, right now, Steve? Don't you want to celebrate a little bit?" asked the mayor.

"No, I gotta get on this right away," I replied.

"You've just earned an incredible victory. We should party a bit, Steve. Cindy is already a zombie, it doesn't get any worse than that," said Bob.

"I'm sorry, I can't stand to see her like this. The longer she's a zombie, the worse I feel. I wanna fix this now," I said and took off running to the east.

The villagers watched me run off into the distance. They were sad to see me go, but they understood why.

"Good luck, Steve," yelled Emily.

I only ran for a short distance, then fell over due to exhaustion. I think I must have hit my limit. I blacked out after that.

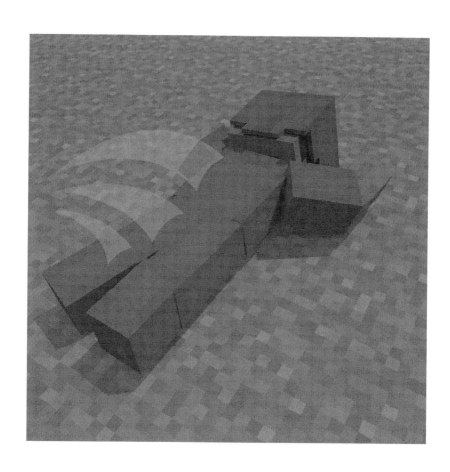

Tuesday

I woke up the next day in a familiar bed. I looked around and realized that I was in Bob's house. Emily was sitting nearby.

"Emily?" I said weakly.

"Steve, you're awake," she said.

"What happened? Why am I here?"

"I think your body gave out and you fainted. You must have overexerted your body."

I sat up and then stood up. "Ow! My legs…they are so sore."

"That must be from sprinting so much the other day."

"The other day? You mean yesterday?"

"No…you slept for three nights."

"What?!" I yelled. "How is Cindy?! Is she okay?"

"Don't worry, Steve. She is fine, I mean, she's still a zombie, but nothing has changed since you knocked out."

"Oh, okay…" I started wobbling towards the door.

"Where are you going?"

"I'm gonna go see the witchhhhh…" I replied as I fell over. My legs gave out.

"Steve, you're in no condition to travel right now. What if you run into a creeper? You would get blown to bits because you can't run away."

I stopped and thought about what Emily said.

"Here, eat some vegetables and get your strength back. You'll need energy if you are to fix Cindy's condition."

I lowered my head and crawled towards the dining table. "I guess you're right…"

The mayor stopped by later that day.

"Steve, how are you today?"

"I'm doing okay, I guess."

"Good. Rest as long as you need to. It is unfortunate that Cindy is a zombie, but she can stand to wait a little while longer."

I looked down. "Do you think I can go visit her?"

"Visit her? She doesn't remember who you are, there would be no point in it."

"I know...but I want to see her," I said.

The mayor and Emily looked at each other.

"I'll need your help, I can't seem to walk properly just yet."

"Okay, Steve. We'll help you get there," said the mayor.

The mayor and Emily assisted me by putting my arms over their shoulders. We walked to my house, which was right down the street. When we got there, I noticed a terrible stench in the air.

I looked at the mayor and Emily and they had covered both their noses.

"What's that smell?" I asked.

The mayor looked at Emily nervously. "Umm…that's—"

"That's n-nothing. I-I don't smell anything…" said Emily.

"Uh…how can you not smell that? It is like super stinky. It smells like rotten vegetables mixed with well-used gym socks," I said.

Then we arrived at my house and I looked inside. I saw Cindy lurking in the corner, and I realized where the smell was coming from. "Cindy…"

"Sorry, Steve. I guess not bathing, not brushing her teeth, and being a zombie trapped in a small confining space has done this to Cindy," said the mayor.

Raggggghhh!

We all looked in the house. Cindy was roaming around bumping into the walls.

"Cindy?" I asked.

She did not reply.

I stood there watching her for a few minutes.

"I've seen enough…let's go…" I said sadly.

We returned home and I sat on my bed.

"Don't be too sad, Steve. I'm sure you'll fix things soon enough," said Emily.

I looked up at her. "I need food. Lots of food."

"Lots of food?"

"Yes, I need to recover as soon as possible. Please give me lots food."

The mayor laughed. "I see. Okay! I'll have Bob cook up a storm for you."

Later that night, Bob returned home from work and cooked up some of the most delicious food ever.

I had steak with potatoes, rabbit stew, pumpkin pie, and some cake. I've never felt so full. The mayor and Emily stayed over for dinner as well.

"Wow, Steve! I've never seen you eat so much," Bob said while laughing.

"Whew! I'm stuffed. I'm trying to make for a fast recovery," I said.

He smiled. "I see. So that was the plan."

"Yep, by tomorrow morning, I should be fully recovered and be able to run around again."

The mayor laughed. "Well, we all should hope so. There is something I've been meaning to talk to you about, Steve."

"What is it, Mr. Mayor?"

"Well, now that you have defeated such a formidable enemy, I was thinking of presenting you with a new title."

"A new title?" I asked curiously.

"Yes, I am thinking about naming you 'Steve the slime slayer.'"

"The slime slayer, eh? That's kind of catchy."

"Oooh! I like it!" said Emily.

"Yeah! That's fancy," added Bob.

I smiled. "It *is* pretty cool."

"I'll hold off on any announcements until later on next week because I know you got things to do," said the mayor. "We will also be throwing a huge banquet in your honor for defeating the slime boss."

"Okay, mayor, it all sounds great," I said.

"Alright, everyone, let's wrap things up. We should let Steve sleep early because he needs to recover," said Bob.

"Thank you, everyone. I'll see you all soon," I said.

I got into bed super early, like maybe around 7 P.M. It was kind of hard to sleep on a super full stomach, but eventually I dozed off.

Wednesday

I woke up during mid-day.

Wow, I guess my body really needed the extra sleep for recovery.

I stood up to check my legs, and to my delight, they were quite normal.

YES! I'm good again. Time to go visit the witch.

On the dining table, I found some food with a note. The note read "Steve, here's some more food for you. Good luck with the witch tomorrow!"

Hmm…that's sweet of Bob, but luck for meeting the witch? What does he mean by that? I wondered.

I grabbed the food and threw it in my bag and headed out the door.

I waved to all the villagers as I passed by.

"Bye, everyone! I'm going to see the witch," I said.

"Oh…good luck, Steve!" yelled Timmy the kid.

Hmm…another person wishing me luck. This might be more of a challenge than I thought.

I headed east and out of town. I had a bag full of food, full leather armor, and my trusty stone sword. I was ready for anything.

"Okay, time to make up for lost time," I said and started sprinting.

I had to travel quickly because it was getting late into the day. According to Emily, the witch's house wasn't too far away.

I was running for about an hour until I saw a higher than normal house made of completely wood. I ran over there as fast as I could.

Upon reaching the door, I was gasping for air.

Whew! My legs and lungs are on fire again. Man, at this rate, I might as well start training for a marathon.

After taking a few minutes to catch my breath, I knocked on the door and waited for a response.

But nothing happened, so I said out loud, "Hello?"

Still, there was no response.

I looked around a bit and then suddenly the door opened violently and a clear flask with some kind of liquid in it was flying towards me.

It hit me directly on the chest and splashed everywhere.

"Ow! What was that?!"

"That's what you get for failing to protect Cindy," said a voice from a dark corner in the house.

"What did you throw at me?!" I asked in a panic.

Then it hit me. My skin started burning like I was on fire.

It was a burning sensation like I have never felt before.

AHHHHHH!!!!

"It burns!!!"

A figure appeared from the dark corner. An older lady dressed in a purple robe. "Good," she said calmly.

"It is so hot! Please help me!!"

She said nothing and just smiled. She looked like she was enjoying the sight of me in excruciating pain.

"AHHHHH!!! I'm on fire!!!"

I remembered something about fire safety

"Stop! Drop! And roll!" I yelled as I rolled all over the ground.

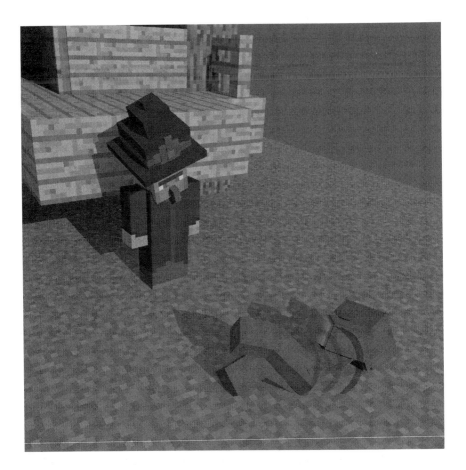

That didn't help at all.

As I rolled helplessly on the ground, the older lady hovered over me, looking down on me.

"You're not on fire," she said calmly.

The burning feeling was slowly subsiding.

I felt like I was close to dying, like I was on my last heart.

As I laid there huffing and panting, the lady kicked me in the stomach.

"Oof! Ugh! Why...?" I asked weakly.

"Cindy was my niece, you jerk."

"Oh..." I replied. It all started to make sense.

I fainted after that...

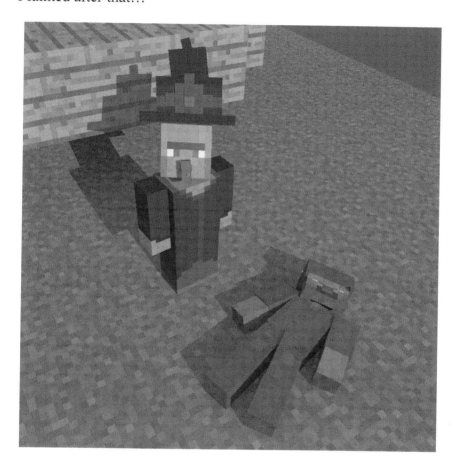

Can You Help Me Out?

Thanks for reading all the way through. I hope that you enjoyed this book. As a new writer, it is hard to get started; it is difficult to find an audience that wants to read my books. There are millions of books out there and sometimes it is super hard to find one specific book. But that's where you come in! You can help other readers find my books by leaving a simple review. It doesn't have to be a lengthy or well written review; it just has to be a few words and then click on the stars. It would take less than 5 minutes.

Seriously, that would help me so much, you don't even realize it. Every time I get a review, good or bad, it just fills me with motivation to keep on writing. It is a great feeling to know that somewhere out there, there are people who actually enjoy reading my books. Anyway, I would super appreciate it, thanks.

If you see new books from me in the future, you will know that I wrote them because of your support. Thank you for supporting my work.

Special thanks again to previous readers and reviewers. Thank you for encouraging me to keep writing. I'll do my best to provide high quality books for you all.

My Other Books

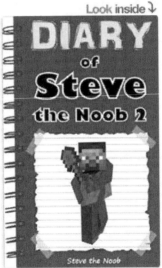

My Awesome List of Favorite Readers and Reviewers

Jewel Shine

Minoscreeperslayer

RainbowCreeper

Sang Chul Choi

Misahti

Panisara W.

Astro Cat

AthanEnder

betsy

akaherobrine

James

Xaxier Edwards

leann xiao

Awesomeguy27

IsaBear556

Emma Hogan

Brandon Kim

Venu Gopal

Kathy

Yuan Cui

Sreekant Gottimukkala

Emma

Kayla Dingo

76624894R00037

Made in the USA
Lexington, KY
21 December 2017